TOP DOG!

BOOKS IN THE PUPPY PATROL™ SERIES

1. *TEACHER'S PET*
2. *BIG BEN*
3. *ABANDONED!*
4. *DOUBLE TROUBLE*
5. *STAR PAWS*
6. *TUG OF LOVE*
7. *SAVING SKYE*
8. *TUFF'S LUCK*
9. *RED ALERT*
10. *THE GREAT ESCAPE*
11. *PERFECT PUPPY*
12. *SAM AND DELILAH*
13. *THE SEA DOG*
14. *PUPPY SCHOOL*
15. *A WINTER'S TALE*
16. *PUPPY LOVE*
17. *BEST OF FRIENDS*
18. *KING OF THE CASTLE*
19. *POSH PUP*
20. *CHARLIE'S CHOICE*
21. *THE PUPPY PROJECT*
22. *SUPERDOG!*
23. *SHERLOCK'S HOME*
24. *FOREVER SAM*
25. *MILLY'S TRIUMPH*
26. *THE SNOW DOG*
27. *BOOMERANG BOB*
28. *WILLOW'S WOODS*
29. *DOGNAPPED!*
30. *PUPPY POWER!*
31. *TWO'S COMPANY*
32. *DIGGER'S TREASURE*
33. *HOMEWARD BOUND*
34. *THE PUPPY EXPRESS*
35. *ORPHAN PUPPY*
36. *BARNEY'S RESCUE*
37. *LOST AND FOUND*
38. *TOP DOG!*

COMING SOON!

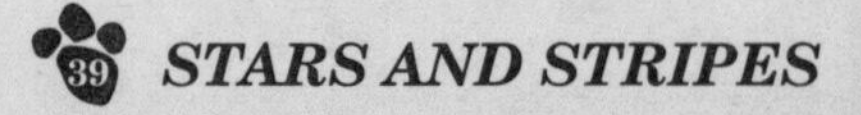

39. *STARS AND STRIPES*

TM

TOP DOG!

JENNY DALE

Illustrations by Mick Reid

Cover illustration by Michael Rowe

AN

APPLE

PAPERBACK

SCHOLASTIC INC.

New York Toronto London Auckland Sydney

Mexico City New Delhi Hong Kong Buenos Aires

ISBN 0-439-54360-6

12 11 10 9 8 7 6 4 5 6 7 8/0

Printed in the U.S.A.
First Scholastic printing, September 2003

CHAPTER ONE

"Look, Em. The Statue of Liberty!" Neil Parker pointed out of the airplane window as the huge jet flew over New York City on its approach to Newark International Airport.

"And that must be Central Park," said his younger sister, ten-year-old Emily. She was leaning toward the cabin window as far as her seat belt would allow, so that she, too, could get a view of the sprawling city below.

Neil looked down at the vast green rectangle dotted with sparkling lakes and surrounded by tall buildings. He grinned. "Looks like an awesome place to walk dogs!"

Emily laughed. "I *knew* you were going to say that!"

Neil was crazy about dogs. Back at home, his whole

life revolved around them. His parents, Bob and Carole Parker, ran King Street Kennels — a boarding kennel and rescue center in the English country town of Compton.

For the umpteenth time since the plane had taken off from Gatwick Airport, Neil found himself thinking about the kennel and his own dog, a young Border collie named Jake. He already missed Jake, but he knew that the dog would be in good hands while he and Emily were in the United States for the summer.

Neil and Emily's first stop was New York, where they'd be spending a week with their old neighbors, Jane and Richard Hammond. The Hammonds used to own Old Mill Farm, which bordered the kennel.

Neil's ears popped as the jet made its final descent. Almost without warning, it hit the ground with a bone-shaking shudder. Eleven-year-old Neil felt a rush of exhilaration as the enormous plane hurtled down the runway, its engines screaming as the pilot applied the brakes.

Gradually, the plane slowed down, then taxied across to the terminal. The voice of the captain came over the loudspeakers. "This is Captain Johnson. We've just landed at Newark International Airport and we hope you've enjoyed the flight. The temperature outside is eighty-two degrees Fahrenheit and the local time is 4:30 P.M."

Neil looked at his watch. It was still set on British time, 9:30 P.M. "Just think, Em," he said, adjusting the watch to American time, "we left home at two o'clock this afternoon and we've been flying for seven-and-a-half hours, but now it's only two-and-a-half hours later than when we left!"

Emily looked puzzled. She yawned. "I don't care what the time is here — my eyes are telling me that it's nearly bedtime!"

"I don't think you'll get to bed until after midnight, British time!" Neil exclaimed. "And then when we wake up tomorrow we'll be suffering from jet lag." He remembered how tired he had felt when, on another vacation, they had arrived in Australia and had actually found themselves ahead of time.

Inside the terminal, the flight attendant who was looking after them helped them find their suitcases at the baggage claim. As they joined the line waiting to go through customs, Neil noticed a uniformed man and a black spaniel walking through the crowds of travelers. "Look — a bomb-sniffing dog," he said to Emily.

The spaniel stopped every now and then to smell a suitcase or a bag before padding off to another set of luggage.

"What do you think he's looking for?" asked Emily.

Neil shrugged. "I dunno. Drugs, maybe?" Fascinated, he watched the spaniel working to detect the faintest whiff of anything illegal that could be hidden in the baggage. It always amazed Neil how smart dogs were. They could be trained to do so many fan-

tastic things that no human could do. No wonder people called them man's best friend.

The customs official waved them through and they entered a vast, crowded arrivals hall.

"Now we're really in America," said Neil happily. He looked around for Jane, who had promised to meet them.

"Neil! Emily!" They could hear Jane's familiar voice before they could see her. Then they spotted the short young woman pushing her way through the crowds and hurrying over to them.

"It's great to see you two again," she said, hugging them warmly. "We've really missed you."

Jane's husband, Richard, had taken a job teaching at an agricultural college in New York. They had bought a house in a suburb near the college and had settled there with their Border collie, Delilah.

"Where's Delilah?" asked Neil, almost before Jane had finished speaking. "Is she in the car?" He was looking forward to seeing the lively collie again, especially since she was Jake's mother.

Jane laughed. "Well, you haven't changed a bit," she said to Neil. "Lost none of your passion for dogs, I see!" Jane explained that she'd left Delilah at home. "Richard needed the car today, so I took a taxi. I thought it would be easier if I left Delilah behind."

They thanked the flight attendant and then went through an exit which led to the taxi stand. A long line of yellow cars waited at the side of the narrow roadway. Jane stood on the curb and held out her arm, and the first taxi in the row pulled out and drove up.

"Hey, look!" exclaimed Neil. "There's a dog in there!"

A big, black Labrador was leaning out of the front right-hand window, his pink tongue lolling out of his mouth. He looked as if he were laughing at them.

"He's gorgeous!" said Emily.

"Can you believe it?" Jane laughed as the driver stowed their luggage in the trunk of the taxi. "Out of the twelve thousand cabs in this city, we *would* get one with a dog in it! Sometimes I think a dog will find you two anywhere!"

They piled into the taxi and Jane leaned forward to speak to the driver through the Plexiglas partition that separated the front of the cab from the back. She told him her address, and the driver was about to slide the plastic across to close the window when the dog pushed his strong head through the gap to inspect the three people in the back.

"Hello, boy." Neil stroked the dog's thick coat, noticing that it was damp and had patches of mud clinging to it in places. *Typical Labrador!* thought Neil. *Can't keep them away from water.*

The dog responded to Neil's touch with a big wet lick across his face. Then he squeezed himself even further through the opening and, with his solid black chest pressing against Neil's face, gave Emily a similar greeting.

"What a big welcome! Does he always do this to passengers?" A mouthful of fur muffled Neil's question.

The driver gently took hold of the dog's collar and pulled him back into the front compartment. "No — first time," he answered. "But then, it's also his first time in my cab. Sit, boy," he said firmly.

The dog obediently sat on the seat next to the driver and looked ahead of him, through the windshield.

"Did you just get him?" asked Emily.

"Yeah, you could say that," the driver said. "He's not mine, actually. I found him running loose, just this morning, so I picked him up before he got hit or caused an accident."

"Where did you find him?" asked Jane.

The driver started the meter, then pulled away from the curb. "In Manhattan. At the south entrance to Central Park," he said as they left the taxi stand and joined the heavy airport traffic. "I'd just dropped off a passenger at the Plaza Hotel and was pulling away to come back to the airport when pandemonium broke out on 59th Street, which runs between the hotel and the park."

His eyes were fixed on the busy road ahead of him, but he spoke loudly so that his passengers could hear. "There's always a lot of honking and hollering in the city, but this was kinda different from the everyday noise. Cars were screeching to a halt and nearly crashing into each other —" He braked sharply, pressing the cab's horn as another yellow taxi suddenly veered in front of them. "No manners," he muttered, releasing the horn.

"What was going on?" asked Emily.

"This dog was running in and out of the traffic, with his leash dragging behind him," replied the driver. "And it wasn't the first time, either — the doorman at the Plaza said he saw the same dog running across from the park last night."

"Poor thing," said Jane. "He must have been desperate."

The driver nodded. "And hungry! He got to the sidewalk, then started rooting around for food in the garbage cans and sniffing around the horse-drawn carriages outside the hotel. He looked pretty rundown but otherwise healthy, so I was sure he was lost and not just a stray — especially since he was wearing a collar."

"Isn't there a name tag and telephone number on it?" asked Neil.

"Nope! No identification at all," replied the driver. He stopped at a set of traffic lights and pet the dog, who was leaning out of the window, panting slightly. "What did you do, boy? Sneak away from your owner to chase a squirrel in the park, then get lost?"

Responding to the driver's touch, the dog drew himself back inside the cab and sat down, his heavy tail thumping against the seat.

"How did you get him into your taxi?" asked Neil. He knew that getting hold of a traumatized dog was never an easy thing to do.

The driver pulled a strip of dried meat out of his pocket and held it up for everyone to see. As if by magic command, the dog spun around and caught hold of the tough-looking meat, then sat chewing it contentedly. "Jerky!" The driver chuckled. "Dogs can't resist it. I got out of my cab and lured him with a stick of it."

"He looks quite settled and happy now," said Jane. "Are you going to take him home?"

"I wish I could, but I'm not allowed to have pets in my apartment," said the driver, accelerating as the lights changed to green. "And I'm pretty sure his owners will be looking for him. They'll probably start by going to the animal shelter, so I'll take him there just as soon as my shift's over today."

"Maybe, instead of a name tag, he's got a microchip under his skin," suggested Neil. "Then his owners can be traced quite easily."

"*If* he has a microchip," emphasized Jane.

"Let's hope he does," said Emily. "It must be hard to tell one pitch-black Labrador from another!"

After about forty minutes, the chaotic rush-hour traffic eased a little and they found themselves driving alongside a wide river through a quiet, leafy suburb.

"The Hudson River," Jane pointed out. "On the other side is New York City itself. Look, you can see the tall skyscrapers of Manhattan."

Neil gazed out of his window at the Manhattan skyline and wondered where, in that huge concrete jungle, the dog's owners were. How lucky for the dog that someone who cared had come to his rescue. It would have been hard for him to fend for himself in such a busy city.

They drove down streets that were lined with neat houses set in small gardens. After a while, the driver turned onto a road marked Fairhaven Avenue.

"Here we are," said Jane, and the cab pulled up outside a white clapboard house.

The driver got out and hauled the luggage onto the pavement. While Jane paid the fare, Neil and Emily said good-bye to the dog, who was craning his neck out of the window once more.

"I'm sure your owner will find you," Neil said, massaging the folds of skin on the dog's chest and neck. "No one would want to lose a nice boy like you." The dog whined softly and licked Neil's arm. "If you were mine, I'd do everything I could to find you."

The driver started the engine, but before he could drive off, Neil leaned through the window to ask him if they could phone to find out how things worked out with the dog.

"Sure thing," replied the driver. "Like I said, after my shift I'll check with the animal shelter to see if his owners have turned up. So why don't you give me a call later tomorrow?" He pulled a business card out of his pocket and handed it to Neil. Below the name and telephone number of the taxi company was the driver's name — Stan Schneider.

"Oh, and please call me, too, if you need a ride anywhere again," added Stan. "It made my day to drive some fellow dog lovers!" He flicked the switch that lit up the numbers on the roof to let people know that

the cab was empty. Then he drove off slowly, with the dog hanging out of the window.

"Bye," called Neil, and the Labrador responded with a short, sharp bark before he dived back inside the cab and disappeared from view.

CHAPTER TWO

Neil watched until the taxi turned a corner, then he picked up his bag and followed Jane and Emily to the front door. As soon as Jane put her key in the lock, the curtains at the window parted and a striking black-and-white face peered out.

"Delilah!" exclaimed Neil.

The Border collie looked as if she could hardly contain her excitement. She started to bounce up and down at the window, barking gleefully.

"Something tells me she recognizes you." Jane laughed. She opened the door and Delilah shot out and tumbled around them like a whirlwind. "OK, calm down now, Delilah," Jane urged the exuberant dog.

But Delilah didn't calm down. She leaped up at

Neil, almost knocking him over, and, with her front paws resting on his shoulders, licked him all over his face.

Neil staggered back a few paces to regain his balance. "*Another* face wash!" he laughed, remembering the greeting the Labrador had given him.

Delilah jumped down off Neil and turned her attention to Emily. She spun around in tight circles, then flopped down at Emily's feet and rolled over onto her back.

Emily kneeled down and tickled the collie's white chest and tummy. "Let's see if this helps to calm you down," she said, grinning.

Neil bent down beside his sister and scratched the panting dog's chest. Delilah reminded him so much of Jake — she had the same smiling eyes and friendly expression. He was glad that he'd have Delilah to help take his mind off Jake while they were in New York. And they'd meet more dogs next week, when they went to Hollywood to stay with their friend, Max.

"Well, we can stay out here all day, or we can go in and have something to drink," teased Jane, who was standing to one side, watching the happy reunion.

Inside the house, Jane showed them to their room upstairs. "There's only the one spare room, so I'm afraid you'll have to share," she said, opening the door to a cheerfully decorated bedroom that looked out on the backyard.

"That's OK," said Emily, yawning and looking longingly at the beds. "We're used to sharing when we're on vacation."

"Yes, I know. But what I really meant was that you'll have to share with Delilah — she's claimed this room as her own!" Jane laughed. She pointed to a big wicker basket on the floor beside one of the beds. A plump cushion lined the basket, and several shabby stuffed animals and a chewed-up Frisbee lay scattered around it.

"All right!" Neil grinned.

Jane left them to unpack and went downstairs. The Border collie stayed with Neil and Emily, sniffing their bags inquisitively.

"Do you think she can smell Jake?" asked Emily.

"Maybe," said Neil.

"Hmm . . . or maybe she's looking for this!" Emily pulled a packet of dog biscuits out of her bag.

But before Emily could give the collie the present she'd brought her, Delilah suddenly sat bolt upright and pricked up her ears. She listened for barely a second, then hurtled to the door and bounded downstairs.

"Hey! What's going on?" said Neil, making his way toward the landing.

He soon got his answer. Richard's voice came up to them from the hall. "Hi there, you two."

Neil and Emily abandoned their half-unpacked bags and went down to say hello.

"Welcome to the Big Apple," the tall, blond-haired man said as he hugged Emily and shook Neil's hand. "Did you have a good flight?"

"It was really cool," said Neil, following Richard into the living room. "Especially when we came in to land. We flew right over New York and saw the whole city."

"You didn't by any chance see this dog from up there?" joked Richard. He pulled a newspaper out of his briefcase. "I think you two might be interested in this story." He pointed to a photograph of a black Labrador on the front page. Standing next to the dog was a man dressed in baseball gear, and above the photograph was a headline that read, "Mets Mascot Missing!"

"Hey, that looks just like . . ." Neil paused, then added, "No — it's not the taxi dog. This one's got a white star on his chest."

Neil scanned the story quickly, then read aloud the most important points. *"Joe, the Mets baseball team's mascot, is missing for the second time,"* he read. *"The first time was three days ago, when the Atlanta Braves stole the dog to lower their rival team's morale."*

"So what happened to him this time?" asked Jane, who had come in from the kitchen with a tray of iced tea and cookies.

"Well, it says here that the Braves were going to return him after the exhibition game between the two teams this week. But he ran off while one of the players was walking him in Central Park early yesterday," explained Neil.

"And no one's found him?" Jane frowned. "How odd." She shook her head, then put the tray on a table and began pouring the tea into glasses.

"I think the article says that someone did catch sight of him," said Richard, handing out the tea. "Isn't that right, Neil?"

"Yeah," said Neil. *"A bystander reported seeing Joe in the park near the zoo gates,"* he read. *"But all attempts to find the famous mascot have failed. The Mets have appealed to people to be on the lookout for Joe. He has a distinctive white star on his chest."*

For the second time that day, Neil found himself thinking how tough it must be for a lost dog on its own in the enormous city.

"What a terrible thing to do to an animal!" said Emily, sounding outraged. "It's as if they're using him as a puppet!"

"Unfortunately, it's all part of the rivalry that goes on between some professional sports teams," said Richard. "Especially now that the baseball season is heating up."

Jane offered everyone a cookie. "Richard's right. You should see the rivalry that's taking place at the moment between the two New York teams, the Mets and the Yankees. They're building up to a really important Major League game on Saturday — the last of three in what they call the 'Subway Series,'" she explained. "No, Delilah — not for you!" Jane gently pushed away the collie, who was sniffing eagerly at the plate of cookies.

"Well, I don't think that's a good excuse to kidnap a dog!" protested Emily. "Especially since the dog can't understand what's going on."

Emily's comment made Neil think about his own dog again. Jake wouldn't be able to understand that Neil would only be away for a few weeks. He hoped that the Border collie didn't miss him. He looked at his watch. It probably wasn't too late to phone home to let Mom and Dad know they'd arrived safely and to find out how Jake was doing.

"Jane, would it be OK if we phoned home quickly?" he asked.

"Sure. I was going to suggest it myself," said Jane. "The phone's in the hall."

Neil and Emily went out into the hall, where Neil picked up the receiver and dialed the long number that would connect them to Compton, all the way across the Atlantic Ocean.

"King Street Kennels."

"Dad!" said Neil. "It's me. We arrived safely."

"Neil! Hello! Are you having a good time?" Bob sounded relieved to hear from them.

"How's Jake?" Neil asked anxiously, ignoring his father's question.

There was a pause, then a chuckle. "It's obvious who matters the most to you! Jake's absolutely fine.

Eating like a whole pack of dogs and as boisterous as ever," Bob reassured him. "Don't you want to know how Mom and I are?"

Neil laughed. "I'm sure you're fine, too!" he said. "I'd better go now, but here's Em. See you soon, Dad." He handed the phone to his sister, who chatted briefly to Bob and Carole. "See you in Alaska in two weeks," she finished.

After their stay in Hollywood, Neil and Emily would be flying to Alaska to meet up with their parents and five-year-old sister, Sarah, for the final week of their vacation. They were going to stay at a husky dog retirement center run by their long-lost relatives, the Simpson family. Neil could hardly wait.

Back in the living room, Richard had turned on the early evening television news. Neil and Emily were just in time to catch a report on the missing dog.

The television reporter confirmed that there was still no sign of the mascot. Then he introduced Mike Maitland, who was Joe's owner. The cameras panned over to Mike, and Neil recognized him as the man in the photograph on the front page of the newspaper.

"If anyone has my dog, please bring him back. We won't press charges or ask any questions — just as long as you return him in good condition," appealed Mike. *"And if anyone knows of a dog that fits Joe's description, please contact me. He's a really friendly guy — pretty energetic most of the time — and as crazy about baseball as the rest of us! He'll go for any ball if he gets the chance. That's why we named him after the great Joe DiMaggio!"*

Neil was startled by that last bit of information. He'd read all about the legendary baseball player in the airline magazine during the flight over. What a coincidence!

"You really can't mistake Joe," Mike continued. *"He has a very glossy black coat and you notice the white star on his chest almost before you notice the rest of him."*

The reporter then introduced a second guest — the member of the Atlanta Braves who had taken Joe from the Mets' locker room as a joke.

The man apologized to Joe's owner, then repeated the appeal for the public to come forward with any information that could lead to the return of the dog. *"We were going to bring back Joe after the game on Thursday and are really sorry this happened,"* he said. *"We like Joe almost as much as his own team does, so we're offering a generous reward to anyone who can bring the dog back."*

When the player finished making his appeal, Richard switched off the television set. "Well, that should do it," he said. "With the promise of a nice sum of money, someone's bound to find Joe very soon!"

"Let's hope so," said Jane. "I know just how desperate his owner must be feeling."

Neil thought back to the time when Delilah had disappeared for a few days during a serious flood in Compton. Jane had been a nervous wreck.

"I don't know what I'd do if Delilah disappeared in New York," continued Jane. "That's why I always keep a tight rein on her when we're out walking in the park — and on all the other dogs."

"What other dogs?" asked Neil, looking confused.

"Aha! I haven't told you about my new job yet, have I?" said Jane mysteriously. "You two will love it. I'm a professional dog walker!"

"A *professional* dog walker?" echoed Emily. "You mean that's a real job over here?"

"Yes," said Jane. "There are lots of dogs in Manhattan whose owners don't have the time or energy to walk them. I'm one of a number of walkers who pick up these dogs from their apartments every day and take them to Central Park for an hour or so."

"Wow!" exclaimed Neil. "Sounds like the perfect job to me!"

"I love it," Jane agreed.

Later, as they all dug into some juicy burgers Richard had prepared for dinner, they discussed plans for the week ahead. "A week doesn't give us a lot of time to see everything in New York," Jane said. "But we'll do as much as we can. Now, since you're both such animal lovers, I suggest we start with the zoo in Central Park tomorrow morning."

Emily frowned. "I hope the animals are in decent-sized pens," she said warily.

Neil smiled at his younger sister. He admired the way she was always concerned about animal rights. If the zoo animals were cooped up in tiny cages, she'd probably refuse to go. But Jane reassured her that, on the whole, the pens were spacious.

"Good," said Neil. "Because I really want to go to the zoo. We might be able to get a lead on Joe there."

Everyone gave him puzzled looks.

"What makes you think that?" asked Jane.

"Well, the article in the newspaper said that the last time someone saw Joe he was near the zoo. I know he won't still be there, but at least it's a starting point."

Neil knew that if they were to have any chance of finding the famous mascot, they'd have to follow any and every clue — no matter how small it seemed.

"What are these?" asked Neil at breakfast the next morning. He was pointing to a plate of hard, ring-shaped bread rolls.

"Bagels," said Jane. "As common in New York as fish-and-chips are in Compton! Try one with some of this jam — or should I say *jelly*?"

"Bagels and jelly! An American version of toast and marmalade!" Emily grinned and helped herself to one of the bagels.

After breakfast, Jane suggested that they leave for the zoo right away so that she would be able to fit in her dog-walking duties afterward. "I'll see if Stan Schneider is available to take us," she said, going into the hall to phone the cab company.

"Great!" said Neil. "Then we can find out if anyone's claimed the Labrador yet."

"Half an hour later, a horn sounded from the street. Delilah leaped up and dashed over to the window, barking excitedly. She glanced back toward Jane, yapping even more urgently, as if trying to tell her something.

"OK, Delilah, I'm coming," said Jane, as she walked out of the kitchen. "I'm sure it's only Stan."

The collie wagged her shaggy tail, then stared out into the street again and continued her high-pitched barking.

Neil and Emily went over to the window to see what was exciting Delilah so much. A yellow cab was

parked in the driveway and Stan was walking up the pavement. But he was not alone.

"Hey! The dog's still with him," cried Neil. "I wonder what happened?"

The Labrador was trotting happily on his leash next to Stan. His ears pricked up at the sound of Delilah's frantic barking.

"Let's find out," said Jane, opening the door.

In a flash, Delilah sprang across and tried to squeeze through the door. "Whoa! You're not going anywhere," said Jane. But the Border collie was too agile for her. She slipped past and hurtled down the path to meet the Labrador.

By the time Neil, Emily, and Jane had caught up with Delilah, the two dogs were sniffing each other in greeting.

"Morning, everyone," said Stan.

"Morning," said Jane in return. She bent down to grasp Delilah's collar, but the two dogs seemed to decide at that very moment that it was time for a game.

Delilah jumped out of Jane's reach, then bowed down in front of the other dog. With her haunches raised, she gazed directly at the Labrador and yapped at him, daring him to meet her challenge. The Labrador, restrained by his leash, could do little more than bark back at her and bounce forward a few steps. Delilah jumped up and pranced from side to side, then bowed down again in front of the

Labrador. The black dog strained hard at the end of his leash, trying to free himself for some roughhousing with his new friend.

"That's enough, Delilah," Jane said with a laugh, managing at last to grab hold of her collar. She led her back toward the house. "I won't be a minute. I'll take her into the backyard."

The Labrador whined softly as he watched Delilah leave. Neil crouched in front of him. "I didn't think we'd see you again," he said, scratching the dog's chest. He looked up at Stan. "How come you've still got him with you?"

"The animal shelter was already closed by the time I got there last night," explained Stan. "So I had to take him home with me."

The Labrador looked up at Stan and wagged his tail contentedly. Stan patted his head. "And now he thinks I'm his best buddy — especially after sharing my dinner and breakfast, and gnawing on a big bone all night."

"I thought you said you weren't allowed to have animals in your apartment," commented Emily, looking puzzled.

"That's right," said Stan. "But I couldn't just abandon him, so I broke the rules and snuck him in."

Neil beamed at the driver in appreciation. It was just the sort of thing he would have done!

Jane returned and Emily filled her in on what they'd just learned.

"So, what's your plan now?" Jane asked the cab driver.

"I was about to take him to the animal shelter when I got your call this morning," said Stan, holding the front door of the cab open for the dog. Without hesitation, the Labrador jumped onto the front seat, then poked his head through the partition to watch the passengers get into the back of the cab. "The shelter is really close to Central Park Zoo, so when I heard that you wanted to go there, I decided to pick you up first. This way I won't have to make two trips in the same direction," he continued, starting up the engine.

Once the taxi was moving, the dog settled down quietly in his place, looking out of the window at the passing sights. They crossed the George Washington Bridge, which spans the Hudson River, and soon found themselves in the seething traffic of Manhattan. Neil stared out at the towering skyscrapers on either side of the road and felt dwarfed by them. Looking upward, he couldn't even see the tops of the buildings.

The Labrador was now almost asleep. He sat sideways, leaning against the back of the seat, with his eyes half-closed. It was almost as if he was so used to the busy city that he found it boring.

"He's really relaxed," said Neil, grinning. "Especially for a lost dog."

"Mmm," agreed Emily. "He's obviously been properly socialized and well trained. It's just too bad his owner didn't think to put a name tag and telephone number on his collar."

"Well, we can't do anything about a phone number," said Neil. "But we can give him a name — even if it's just a temporary one."

"OK," said Emily. "Any ideas?"

Neil thought for a moment. The Labrador seemed to be so much at home in New York. His new name should reflect that. "I've got it," he declared. "We'll call him Bagel!"

"Perfect!" said Emily enthusiastically. She leaned through the partition. "What do you think of that, Bagel?"

The dog opened his eyes and cocked his head, first to one side and then to the other. He panted slightly, then gave a single, low bark.

Neil laughed. "I think he likes it."

Soon the cab turned onto a wide avenue flanked by tall trees. Jane explained that they were crossing Central Park and heading for the zoo, which was at the southern end of the park.

The sight of the leafy surroundings seemed to excite Bagel. Fully alert once more, he leaned forward, staring intently through the windshield and trembling slightly.

"Perhaps he recognizes the park and thinks he's going for a walk," said Emily.

"Maybe he's hoping to see his owner," suggested Neil.

Bagel was now standing on the seat, his sharp eyes fixed on something in the distance. Suddenly, he began to bark hysterically.

"Hey! What's up, boy?" said Stan, slowing down and reaching across to Bagel in an attempt to get him to sit quietly.

Bagel hardly noticed Stan's calming gesture. Thrusting forward, he put his front paws on the dashboard and began to snarl ferociously in between bursts of loud barking.

"What's wrong, Bagel?" Neil leaned through the partition and rubbed the Labrador's straining flank muscles.

But Bagel was oblivious to everything except whatever it was that had caught his eye.

"He's never behaved like this before," yelled Stan in confusion, shouting to be heard above the barking. "I can't concentrate. I'll have to find a place to pull over until he calms down."

There was a solid line of traffic on both sides of the avenue, making it difficult for Stan to stop. An impatient driver behind them honked at the slow-moving taxi. Stan moved over as close to the curb as he could to give the car a chance to overtake them, then rejoined the traffic.

Just then, Neil spotted what was upsetting Bagel.

Not far in front, on a path up an embankment that ran alongside the road, was a woman with several dogs. "Look! There's the problem," he cried, pointing to the tall, red-haired woman and the three dogs with her. "He's seen those dogs."

Bagel's front feet clawed at the dashboard and the hair on his back was raised threateningly in a stiff ridge. Neil couldn't believe the sudden change in him — especially since he hadn't been at all vicious when he met Delilah.

The cab, still moving slowly, was now almost parallel with the woman. She was heading for a footbridge that crossed the road when her dogs, hearing the loud barking behind them, started straining at

their leashes. The woman yanked the leashes, then turned around to see where all the noise was coming from. In that instant, Bagel dived to the floor, knocking Stan's arm and making him lose control of the cab for a moment.

"Hey!" shouted Stan as the car veered to the side of the road. With a loud crunch, it crashed into a lamppost on the curb.

"Oh no!" cried Jane in alarm. They found themselves being rammed backward into their seats, then jerked forward as the cab lurched to a halt.

Neil felt the air being knocked out of him. "Oof!" he gasped.

"Are you all right?" Jane asked anxiously, turning quickly to Neil and Emily.

"I . . . I think so," said Emily, her eyes wide with shock at the sudden impact.

Neil leaned forward to see how Stan and Bagel were. The driver was clearly more worried than harmed. "Now look what you've gone and done," he was saying to Bagel, who was cringing on the floor, breathing heavily. Bagel looked up at Stan and whimpered. The driver shook his head. "OK, fella, I know you didn't do it on purpose. But you shouldn't have been jumping around like that." He sighed, then pushed open his door and got out to inspect the damage.

Neil quickly slid out onto the pavement. "I'll just check that Bagel's not hurt," he said.

Already, a row of traffic was backed up behind them and a small group of curious spectators had gathered on the path to see what was going on. "Need any help?" someone called out as Neil was about to open Bagel's door. "Is anyone injured?"

Neil turned to answer, but before he could speak Bagel jumped up. With one swift leap, the dog shot out of Stan's open door. As if in a blind panic, he charged across the road, narrowly avoiding a car coming from the opposite direction. He clambered frantically up the steep bank on the other side of the road, then disappeared into the undergrowth.

"Bagel!" yelled Neil. "Come back!" He glanced up and down the avenue, and as soon as there was a gap in the traffic, he dashed off after the Labrador. Scrambling up the bank, he had just one thought. He *couldn't* let the terrified dog get lost again in this huge park. Neil knew he had to find him — and fast!

CHAPTER FOUR

At the top of the embankment, Neil paused to catch his breath. He looked around, trying to figure out which way Bagel would have gone. A wide path zig-zagged through clumps of dense bushes toward a wooded area. Would the Labrador have kept to the path, making for the woods, or would he have taken cover in the bushes?

Probably the path, Neil decided quickly. *He'd head away from the road.* He started to run along the path, his eyes scanning the surroundings for any sign of Bagel.

"Wait for me!"

Neil glanced over his shoulder and saw Emily sprinting toward him. A few yards behind her, Jane was running hard to keep up. Neil slowed down until Emily reached him.

"Where did he go?" she puffed.

"I dunno. Those woods, maybe," said Neil, stepping up his pace again just as Jane caught up with them.

"Slow down a bit," she pleaded breathlessly. "Next thing you know, you'll get lost, too!"

They charged into the woods, disturbing a pair of gray squirrels that scurried across the path and swiftly climbed the nearest tree. A rustling noise in some nearby bushes made Neil spin around. His hopes that it was Bagel were dashed, though, when a large bird broke out from the foliage and flew away.

The path rounded a bend, then suddenly forked — the left fork continuing into the woodland and the right one leading to a grassy expanse where people were picnicking and playing games.

"*Now* which way?" Neil stopped and scratched his head in exasperation. Whichever path they chose, the chances of finding Bagel were beginning to seem very remote. He remembered how big Central Park had looked from the air. Trying to find a frightened dog in it would be a bit like searching for a needle in a haystack.

Before they could make a decision, two teenage boys came along on in-line skates on the path toward them.

"Maybe they've seen him," suggested Emily. "Let's ask."

As the skaters whizzed up, Neil called out to them. The two boys slid expertly to a stop and Neil asked if they'd seen a big black dog running loose.

"Yeah! We did see a black dog," said one of the boys. "But he wasn't really loose. He was with a bunch of small kids playing in the trees back there." He pointed to the woods behind him.

"That could be him," said Neil hopefully. "Thanks, guys." He turned to Emily and Jane. "Let's go!" he said, taking the left-hand fork.

"We shouldn't get our hopes up too much," said Jane as they hurried along the path, looking behind thickets and into the trees beyond. "There must be hundreds of big black dogs in this city."

Neil nodded. "I know." It was likely that the dog would turn out to belong to the children, but it was worth a try.

The path went up a small hill. As they crested it they spotted the group of children playing in a clearing about fifty feet ahead. With them, lying on the ground, was an exhausted-looking Bagel.

Neil took a deep breath. "It *is* him!"

He was just about to call out to the Labrador when a woman coming from the opposite direction cried out, "*There* you are, at last!" She whistled loudly and shouted, "Here boy! Come!"

"Hey, it's the woman we saw earlier. She must have come across the bridge," said Neil, recognizing her three dogs. "Maybe Bagel's *her* dog."

Bagel pricked up his ears. He lifted his head and stared at the woman who had left the path and was approaching him slowly.

"Yes," agreed Emily. "It looks like he knows her."

"*I* know her, too," said Jane. "Her name's Glynnis. She's a professional dog walker. Perhaps Bagel's one of her charges."

They stood on the hill, expecting to see Bagel go dashing toward his handler. The dog got up as Glynnis came closer, but he made no move toward her.

"Come on, boy," the woman coaxed. Her other dogs were yapping excitedly at the sight of Bagel. "Quiet, everyone," she snapped, tugging their leashes. She held out her hand and called to Bagel again. But the Labrador seemed rooted to the spot.

Neil frowned. Why wouldn't Bagel go to her?

Glynnis pulled a leash out of her pocket. "Now, you just get over here," she said firmly. Bagel backed up a few steps. "Hey, kids!" she shouted. "Grab hold of my dog, will you?"

One of the children lunged for the Labrador, but the dog was too quick for her. He turned sharply and ran off toward the trees.

"Bagel!" yelled Neil.

At the sound of Neil's voice, the Labrador stopped dead in his tracks. He cocked his head to one side and listened.

"Here, Bagel," shouted Neil again.

Then, as if he'd made up his mind, Bagel suddenly spun around. Avoiding the woman, he barreled across to Neil and bumped into him with such force that Neil found himself knocked flat on the ground.

"And I'm glad to bump into you again, too!" Neil laughed, looking up at the panting dog. "Quick, Em. Hold onto him before he runs away again."

Emily grasped the Labrador's collar in both hands while Neil got back on his feet. He patted Bagel's broad back. "What was that all about, boy?"

Bagel opened his mouth in a wide smile and wagged his tail happily. It was as if nothing had happened.

"I'm so sorry about that. Are you all right?" At the sound of Glynnis's voice, Bagel immediately stopped wagging his tail. He shrank back against Neil's legs and whined quietly.

"Now what's the matter?" asked Neil, confused by Bagel's sudden mood change.

Bagel started to growl softly as the woman came nearer. Neil noticed that she'd tethered her three dogs to a bench next to the path a few feet back. "Oh, hi, Jane," she said, recognizing her fellow dog walker. "I'm really sorry," she repeated. "I thought for a minute he was mine."

"Isn't he?" asked Jane, perplexed.

"Oh . . . uh . . . no." Glynnis seemed taken aback. "Isn't he yours?"

"No. He's lost," Jane told her. "He was found at the Plaza two days ago and we're trying to find his owner. You wouldn't know anything about him, would you, Glynnis?"

"Well, maybe . . ." The woman took a step toward Bagel, who instantly bristled and growled more loudly. "Now, now, doggy — I won't hurt you," she said.

The Labrador lifted his top lip and snarled at Glynnis.

"Hey! What's the matter, Bagel?" said Neil. "You've never been like this before."

While Neil was speaking, Glynnis looked as if she was about to reach for the dog again, but she suddenly changed her mind. She shook her head firmly. "No," she said. "He's obviously not one of mine. He wouldn't kick up such a fuss if he was. I definitely made a mistake. Mine wasn't a . . . um . . . a complete pedigree like him." She turned and started to walk away, declaring, "I'm afraid I've never seen him before, so I don't have a clue where he's from. Sorry — can't help you."

Bagel glared at the retreating back of the woman and gave one sharp bark. Then he shook himself and sat down calmly at Neil's side.

Neil, Jane, and Emily looked at each other in confusion. "That's really weird," said Neil softly. "I could have sworn he recognized her."

"Me, too," agreed Jane. "Why was he so aggressive toward her if he didn't know her? It doesn't make sense."

Neil had a sudden thought. Maybe Bagel's strange behavior had something to do with the other dogs. There was only one way to find out. "Let's take him to meet her dogs," he said.

With Neil grasping Bagel's collar firmly, they followed Glynnis to where she'd tethered the three dogs — a Standard poodle, a Shih Tzu, and a Boston terrier. Neil could see that they were all very good examples of their breeds. "They're beautiful dogs," he said to Glynnis. "I guess *they're* all pedigrees."

"Yes," muttered Glynnis, bending down to untie the dogs.

"Actually, I've noticed that you generally walk pedigrees," commented Jane.

Glynnis didn't respond to Jane's remark. She seemed too absorbed in untying the leashes.

"Do you mind if we pet them?" asked Emily.

"OK. But only for a moment. I'm in a hurry," came Glynnis's terse reply.

Bagel stood quietly while Glynnis untied the leashes, but when she straightened up and looked at him he growled and flashed his sharp teeth at her again. Neil noticed that as long as Glynnis had her back to him, Bagel didn't mind her presence too much. But as soon as she faced him or came toward him, he became very unsettled.

"That's enough, Bagel," said Jane firmly. She apologized to Glynnis, who smiled weakly. "Maybe he doesn't like my perfume," she said in a brittle voice.

The four dogs approached each other with interest. The poodle stretched forward and sniffed at Bagel. They touched noses, then Bagel licked one of the poodle's ears. The smaller dogs also greeted Bagel, who sniffed them in turn and nudged them gently with his wet nose. But even as he made friends with them, Bagel kept a wary eye on Glynnis.

No problem here, thought Neil. *It's not the dogs — so it's got to be Glynnis who's making Bagel so uptight.* He pet the handsome poodle, then crouched down and made a fuss over the two smaller dogs. The Boston terrier particularly enjoyed the attention. She whirled around, sniffing and grinning at Neil.

"She's like a little clown," chuckled Emily, bending

down to pat the black-and-white terrier. Then she turned her attention to the silky Shih Tzu, who stood proudly to one side, slowing wagging his tail. The tiny dog welcomed Emily's touch and, without warning, jumped into her arms.

"Oh, you're really cute." Emily grinned. "I could take you home with me! Where does he live?" she asked Glynnis.

"Oh, on . . . uh . . . Fifth Avenue," replied Glynnis. Then, abruptly, she added, "Well, I have to go. Nice to meet you all." She reached across to take the Shih Tzu from Emily. "Come on, Fluffy," she said.

The little dog shrank back into Emily's arms. As

Glynnis's hand folded around his collar, he lunged forward and nipped her arm.

"You horrible little beast!" cried Glynnis, pulling her arm away and rubbing the wound.

The Shih Tzu glared at Glynnis, and Neil noticed a look of anger pass across the woman's face. He caught her eye briefly. In a syrupy tone, Glynnis said, "Sorry, Fluffs. Did I pull your hair, my angel?" Ignoring the little dog's low growl, she swiftly took him from Emily, then plonked him roughly on the ground and walked away without a backward glance. The dogs lagged behind, and Glynnis jerked their leashes to get them to speed up.

Neil watched the three dogs walking reluctantly behind her. How unusual for dogs not to want to go for a walk!

"She's so impatient with them," remarked Emily.

"Well, I suppose she's in a hurry," said Jane.

"That doesn't mean she has to be so rough with them," protested Neil as Glynnis disappeared from view.

Jane nodded. "I guess not." She turned and started back up the path. "We'd better get going, too. Poor Stan — we just abandoned him!"

As he walked back through the park, with Bagel loping calmly by his side, Neil couldn't get rid of an uncomfortable feeling in the pit of his stomach. Something was definitely wrong. The dogs had all been unhappy with Glynnis. She didn't seem to understand dogs at all, which was strange considering that her job was to walk them. Neil felt very glad that Glynnis hadn't turned out to be Bagel's owner or handler, after all.

Stan was leaning against the lamppost, staring miserably at the mangled bumper of his taxi. Neil noticed that the wheel was also badly dented. There was no way they'd be driving off in that cab.

"Thank goodness!" exclaimed Stan with relief when he saw them returning with Bagel. "Now the only thing I have to worry about is my boss's reaction to the crash."

"Will he be angry that you had Bagel in the taxi?" asked Neil.

Stan shrugged. "Who knows? But I can tell you one thing — he's not going to be very happy about the damage." He put a hand on Bagel's neck and ruffled his fur. "For a dog that's not mine you're causing me a whole lot of trouble," he said.

Bagel looked up at him and whined softly.

"Oh, all right — you're having a tough time, too," Stan said kindly. "What's done is done. I know you didn't mean any harm. But I still can't figure out why you got so upset."

"I think it has something to do with that dog walker we saw before we crashed," explained Neil. "You should have seen how anxious he got when she came near him." He briefly told Stan what had happened when they went to find Bagel. "So we're no closer to finding his owner, after all," he finished.

"That's a pity," said Stan. "Because I really don't know what I'm going to do with him now." He kicked the damaged wheel. "You see, I have to wait here for a tow truck to take the cab back to the garage."

"So you're wondering how to get Bagel to the animal shelter?" Jane asked.

Stan nodded glumly.

"We can take him for you," offered Jane. "If you can manage to get us another cab," she added.

"Would you?" Stan said gratefully. He flagged down an empty taxi that belonged to the company he worked for, and instructed the driver to take the four passengers to the animal shelter. "And bill me for the fare," he added.

Jane protested, but Stan insisted. "The dog's my responsibility," he said stubbornly. Then he crouched down and wrapped his arms around Bagel's neck. "Bye for now, boy. I'll check up on you, but I'm pretty sure it won't be long before you're back in your own home."

Soon, the cab was heading down the avenue, with Bagel sitting next to Neil. The Labrador gazed miserably out the back window at Stan.

"I think he's sad to be leaving Stan," said Emily.

When he could no longer see the taxi driver, Bagel flopped to the floor and lay his head on Neil's feet. His dark brown eyes drooped mournfully. Nothing that Neil said or did seemed to cheer him up.

The cab left Central Park and entered the busy street that would take them to the animal shelter. The driver opened the glass partition. "Only a few more blocks to go," he said.

Neil, Emily, and Jane looked at one another in silence, and then at Bagel. Neil couldn't remember when he'd last seen a more dejected-looking dog. And the Labrador would probably become even more miserable when he found himself in the unfamiliar surroundings of the animal shelter. If only —

Jane broke into Neil's thoughts. "I wonder if anyone's thinking what I'm thinking?"

Neil raised his eyebrows. "What's that?"

"That Bagel's been through enough and that he should come home with us until we find his owner," said Jane.

"Cool!" Neil was delighted. "That's just what I was hoping."

Jane tapped on the partition. "Um . . . excuse me . . .

we've changed our minds," she said loudly. "We're not going to the animal shelter after all." She told him her address, and the driver immediately changed direction and headed toward the George Washington Bridge.

Bagel perked up almost immediately. He jumped onto the seat between Neil and the door and pushed his head out of the half-open window.

"Well, how about that?" Neil laughed. "He's back to his old cheerful self."

"That's amazing. I think he understands everything!" exclaimed Emily.

Bagel barked happily and swished his long tail rhythmically from side to side, brushing Neil's face in the process. Neil removed a few dog hairs from his mouth. "I wish he could talk, too," he said. "Then he could tell us where he comes from."

"Well, the next best way to find his owner is to put an ad in the "Lost and Found" column in the newspaper," said Jane. "I'll do that as soon as we get back. And I'll call the animal shelter, just in case anyone's been asking about him there."

At home, Jane led Bagel out to the back porch. Delilah was lying at the base of a tall oak tree, watching the squirrels that were scampering about in the branches. She sprang to her feet as soon as Jane opened the porch door, and ran to greet them.

The two dogs met head-on as Delilah was climbing the steps up to the porch and Bagel was making his way down. After hesitating for a moment, they touched noses just long enough to become reacquainted, then tumbled into the garden, where they immediately began a wild and noisy game of tag.

"Take it easy, you two." Jane clapped her hands to try to get their attention. "You'll disturb the neighbors if you keep it up. . . ."

"I think they already have," said Neil, pointing to the yard next door.

A blond-haired girl of about sixteen was peering over the fence and laughing at the sight of the dogs' antics.

"Hi, Casey," called Jane. "Sorry about all the noise and dust."

"Oh, no problem," Casey replied, pushing up the baseball cap she was wearing. "I was just sitting out on the deck trying to get a little tan. I didn't know you had a new dog."

"We don't," Jane told her. "But it's a long story. Why don't you come over for lunch? Then you can meet Neil and Emily and we'll fill you in on the details."

"Great," said Casey. "I'll throw some clothes over my swimsuit and be there in a few minutes."

While they waited for Casey to arrive, Jane called the animal shelter to see if anyone had been looking for Bagel. But so far there had been no reports of a missing dog that fit his description. Jane then phoned the newspaper offices to place an advertisement in the "Lost and Found" column. "Pure black male Labrador found at the south end of Central Park," she dictated, and gave her name and telephone number to the person taking the details. "There. Let's hope that does the trick — and soon," she said, hanging up the phone. "If Bagel's with us for much longer, I'm going to find it hard to part with him."

"So's Delilah," Emily observed with a chuckle as the dogs came panting indoors and flopped down together in the hall to rest.

"And what about Bagel?" added Neil. "He seems to have made himself at home already!"

The Labrador had rolled onto his back, and his legs were sticking straight up in the air. His eyes were closed and he appeared to be fast asleep, but

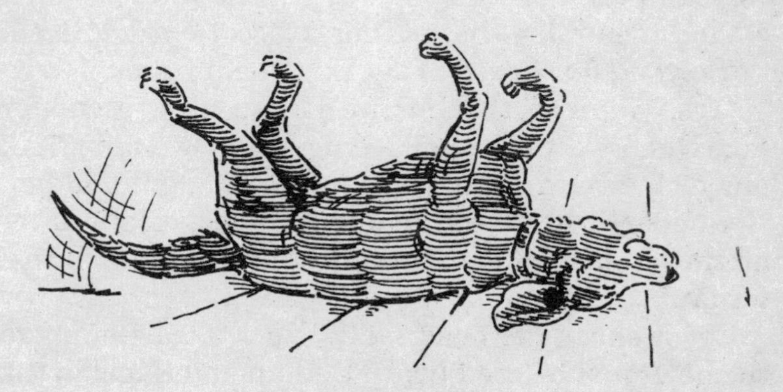

his tail thudded slowly up and down on the wooden floor.

"Silly dog," Jane said fondly.

Later, after Casey had arrived and they were all sitting on the back porch eating hot dogs, Neil told her about Bagel.

Casey was amused to hear how much Neil and Emily had experienced since their arrival in New York less than twenty-four hours before.

"Something you need to know about these two," declared Jane, "is that wherever they are, there's usually a canine drama taking place! I don't know whether they look for the excitement or whether it looks for them."

Casey spread some more ketchup on her hot dog. "In that case," she said, "I'm surprised you're not involved in the other dog mystery."

"You mean Joe the missing mascot?" asked Neil.

"So you *have* heard about him," said Casey.

"Yes. We even thought we'd keep an eye out for him when we were sightseeing — but we didn't get much chance to do that this morning!" Neil told her. "I wonder if he's been found yet — especially after all the publicity and the reward that was offered yesterday."

Casey shook her head sadly. "No, I was listening to the news just before I heard Delilah and Bagel in the yard. There was nothing new. Now I'm really worried about the game on Thursday — as well as the big one on Saturday."

Neil looked at her, puzzled. "Why?"

She picked up her cap, which she'd taken off when she came into the house. "I'm a Mets fan," she explained, pointing to the blue-and-orange logo above the peak.

"Oh, right. And you think they're going to lose without Joe there?" Neil guessed.

Casey nodded.

"I'm sure it's just a matter of time before he's returned," Jane said cheerfully. "All of New York must know about him by now." She stood up. "Ice cream, anyone?"

"Yes, please!" all three of them said enthusiastically. Jane went into the kitchen, with Delilah and Bagel padding behind her.

"You two aren't having ice cream," came her voice from inside. "There are nice crunchy dog biscuits if you want anything." She returned with four large bowls of ice cream and the box of bone-shaped biscuits that Emily had brought from England. The dogs wolfed down their treats, then dashed back into the yard, where the Border collie began to herd the Labrador. Delilah scuttled to one side of the yard, then stopped and crouched, staring intensely at Bagel. After a few moments she began to advance slowly toward him, weaving artfully from side to side.

"She's treating him like a sheep," said Neil.

"And he's totally confused!" Emily laughed.

Bagel was sitting in the middle of the yard, watching Delilah's strange behavior. His face was creased in a frown and he tipped his head first to one side, then to the other. Suddenly, he jumped up and rushed at the collie, completely ruining her herding exercise.

"Well, he's not a very good sheep!" Jane laughed. "But at least the poor squirrels will get a break from her herding."

"And both dogs are getting plenty of exercise," commented Casey.

"Speaking of which, I'm going to have to leave you all now," said Jane, looking at her watch. "I've got some other dogs to exercise."

"Oh yes, of course," remembered Casey. "Your

doggy clients. You've really got your hands full with dogs now."

"Much better than working in an office!" said Jane, with a grin.

While Jane was getting ready upstairs, Casey told Neil and Emily that she was on vacation from school and offered to show them around New York if Jane said it was OK. "That way, she won't have to pack so much into one day, and I'll have a lot of fun taking you to some great places in the city."

"I'd love to go up the Statue of Liberty," said Emily.

"We can do that," Casey said. "And, if you like, I'll take you to a baseball game. Not the big one on Saturday, because it's already sold out, but the exhibition game between the Mets and the Braves on Thursday."

"Sounds good," said Neil enthusiastically. "With any luck, someone will have found Joe by then. Who knows? If we keep our eyes peeled, maybe we'll be the ones to come across him!"

"I wouldn't bet on it," said Casey uncertainly. "If Joe has been stolen by someone hoping to claim the reward, you can be pretty sure he's well hidden."

She was right, Neil thought. The thief wouldn't be careless enough to allow the dog to be seen in public — not now that his photo had been in the papers and on the news. Still, while Joe was missing, there was always a small chance that someone could stumble across him — even if it was in the most unlikely place.

"Don't you think she's about the same age as Saba?" Neil asked Emily.

"Could be," said Emily, gazing at a leopard cub asleep in the branches of a tree in the large leopard enclosure at the Central Park Zoo.

"Who's Saba?" asked Casey.

"My leopard cub in Africa," replied Emily, with a grin.

"You have a leopard cub?" Casey said in disbelief. "You're kidding?"

"No, it's true," said Emily. "Saba's real and, in a way, she really is mine. You see, I sponsor her." She explained about the sponsorship her parents had given her as a present for her tenth birthday. "That way, the wildlife park where Saba lives can afford to take proper care of her — and I get regular updates on how she's doing."

"What a cool gift!" said Casey as they moved on to the next pen.

It was late morning and they'd already been at the zoo for a couple of hours. Casey had met Neil and Emily soon after breakfast and they had taken a train from the Hammonds' house into Manhattan.

The zoo was home to a variety of animals. There were species that Neil and Emily had never seen before, but Neil was particularly drawn to the wolves — mainly because they were so much like dogs.

"Let's get some ice cream," said Casey, spotting a vendor nearby. "And then we'll move on. We've pretty much seen everything here, I think."

Next on their itinerary that day was a boat trip to the Statue of Liberty in New York Harbor.

"We'll take the subway down to Battery Park at the southern tip of Manhattan," explained Casey, licking her ice cream cone, as they headed for the zoo gates. "That's where we buy the tickets for the ferry trip to Liberty Island."

The city was crowded with people who bumped and jostled one another as they hurried along. Every now and then, Neil spotted a dog out on a walk, but even though there were one or two black Labradors, none of them matched Joe's description. One of the Labradors had a white patch on his throat and, for a moment, Neil thought he could be the mascot. Then he remembered Joe's owner emphasizing that the white star on the dog's chest was unmistakable. A patch on the throat was certainly not the same as a star on the chest!

Face it, Neil told himself eventually. *Joe's definitely not going to be walking around the city streets. The next time anyone sees him will be after the thief has claimed the reward.*

Battery Park was full of people waiting to visit the famous statue. Neil, Emily, and Casey joined the line stretching out from the ticket booth. Neil thought they were in for a long, boring wait under the hot sun, but was surprised to find the line moving quickly.

Before long, they boarded the ferry. "Let's go to the front," suggested Neil, and they threaded their way through the groups of tourists to the bow of the boat.

Casey leaned forward and rested her arms on the railings. "We'll get a good view of the statue from here," she said.

The boat's engines began to churn and throb and soon they were gliding out into New York Harbor. A light wind gusted around the bay, whipping up a fine spray which settled on the people standing in the prow.

"That feels good." Neil grinned, grateful for the cool shower after the heat of the city.

As they approached Liberty Island, they stared in awe at the colossal statue of the woman in flowing

robes that loomed before them. On her head was a spiked crown and in her right hand she held up a torch.

"I never thought it was *this* big," said Emily. "Can we go all the way to the top?"

"Yep! Right up to her crown," said Casey.

"Not to her torch?" asked Neil.

"No. The steps go that far, but visitors aren't allowed up," Casey explained. "It's not safe enough."

The boat bumped against the quay and the sight-seers spilled out and began to explore the island and its enormous copper statue. After waiting in yet another line, Neil, Emily, and Casey went inside the statue and began the long climb to the top.

"Race you up," said Neil.

"You must be joking!" Casey laughed. "Do you know how many steps there are?"

"About a thousand?" asked Emily.

"Not quite. Three hundred and fifty-four — to the crown. And that's a lot of steps to run up!" said Casey.

They clattered up the metal stairs, stopping at times to catch their breath.

"Aren't you glad we're not racing?" puffed Emily.

"Very!" said Neil, his chest heaving.

At last they reached the top and stepped out into the viewing gallery inside the spiked crown. All around the wall of the gallery were windows that looked out onto New York Harbor.

"Everything looks so tiny from up here," said Emily.

Far below them, boats that looked like miniatures plowed back and forth on the sparkling waters. Even the skyscrapers that formed the Manhattan skyline to the north of the statue looked smaller.

"Just think, somewhere down there, among all those buildings, is a black dog wondering where his owner is," said Neil.

"*Two* black dogs!" Emily reminded him.

"Oh, right. For a minute I forgot Bagel. But that's because he's not exactly alone!" Neil chuckled. He thought back to that morning, when he had given Delilah and Bagel their breakfast. In typical Labrador fashion, Bagel had wolfed down his food in seconds flat, then sat drooling as he watched Delilah daintily eating hers. If he *had* been upset, he certainly wouldn't have had such a good appetite!

"Hi, everybody. Did you have a good day?" Jane asked them when they arrived home late that afternoon.

"Yes, great!" said Neil. "New York's really cool!"

"Even the zoo?" Jane looked pointedly at Emily. "Did it get your approval?"

Emily smiled. "It was OK. But I wish there were no animals in captivity anywhere. Wild animals should be free to roam as they please," she said wistfully. "Still — I guess they're safe in their pens at least."

"Mmm, safer than black Labradors are in New York," joked Neil. He pet Bagel, who had run in from the backyard with Delilah to see who had arrived.

"Speaking of which," said Jane, "I called Stan to give him the update and I also called the animal shelter again, but no one's asked about a black Lab. Except the Mets, of course. Apparently they also phoned the animal shelter to find out if Joe had been dropped off."

Casey sighed. "So he's *still* missing!" She shook her head. "The game's really not going to be the same without him tomorrow."

"That's what people I spoke to in the park kept saying," Jane commented. "I can tell you something, though," she added with a grin, "if someone *were* to take Joe out, he'd be recognized in a flash. I bumped into lots of Mets fans who were on the lookout for him!"

Neil had an image of a whole army of baseball supporters combing the streets of New York for the missing mascot.

"Oh, and I also bumped into someone else in the park today," Jane continued as they went out to the back porch to have some cold drinks. "Glynnis. I tried to chat with her, but she was a bit unfriendly."

"She wasn't exactly friendly yesterday, either," muttered Emily.

"You're right," agreed Jane. "There's something

about her that makes me uneasy — but I just can't put my finger on it."

"Maybe she's still upset about what happened yesterday," said Neil, patting Bagel, who was sitting in front of him with one paw in his lap. "You *were* a bit strange toward her, weren't you, boy?" he said to the dog.

Bagel barked once at Neil, then pawed at him. "Oh, all right!" Neil laughed. "You're not really strange. But if you weren't uncomfortable around Glynnis yesterday, then I don't know what was going on!"

Jane leaned forward to pat the Labrador. "Yes, for some reason he took an instant dislike to her."

When they had finished their drinks, Casey pushed back her chair. "Well, I'd better head home now. I'll need plenty of rest tonight." She smiled. "We've got a long day ahead of us tomorrow."

"What's tomorrow's program?" asked Jane.

"The *U.S.S. Intrepid* Sea-Air-Space Museum and the Empire State Building in the morning," Emily rattled off.

"And don't forget the baseball game later in the day," said Neil.

"Phew! I feel exhausted just listening to you," Jane declared with a laugh. "Thank goodness for Casey! I don't think I'd have the stamina to fit in half as much in one day."

Later, when Richard came home, Neil headed straight for the newspaper to see if Jane's advertisement had been placed and if there were any reports of a missing dog that fit Bagel's description.

"Your ad's here," he called to Jane as he skimmed the "Lost and Found" column.

"Not that you'd know it," said Jane. "There hasn't been a single call in response to it yet."

"Hey, look at this!" exclaimed Neil. A photograph of a short-muzzled, black-and-white dog had caught his eye. There was a caption that described the dog and stated that the family that owned her was desperate for her to be returned and was offering a generous reward. She was a friendly, much-loved pet.

Neil looked more closely. He had definitely seen the dog before. As he tried to place the dog, suspicion began to form in his mind.

"Mmm, she looks familiar," said Emily, peering over Neil's shoulder. She frowned and chewed at her thumbnail thoughtfully, then burst out, "That's it! She's just like that cute little Boston terrier Glynnis was walking yesterday."

"Exactly!" said Neil, running his eyes down the rest of the column. "I wonder if . . ." He paused, then suddenly punched the air with his fist. "Yes! Listen to this." He read out an advertisement for a missing Shih Tzu. "Isn't that a coincidence?"

Jane frowned at him. "What do you mean?"

"Remember? Glynnis also had a Shih Tzu. I wonder if it could be this one?" he said. His suspicions were now clearer. This just might explain why the three dogs with Glynnis had seemed so uncomfortable with her.

"Now hold on a second," said Richard, pulling the newspaper across to see the advertisements. "Lots of dogs look alike. You can't be sure that these are the same ones that were with Glynnis."

"I think they could be," said Neil confidently. "You see, those dogs definitely didn't like her." He leaned toward the newspaper. "I bet if we keep reading we'll find an ad for a lost Standard poodle! That would definitely prove it."

"Prove what exactly?" asked Richard.

"Who the thief could be," said Neil.

Jane looked at him aghast. "Are you implying that Glynnis —"

"Yes." Neil didn't give Jane time to finish. "I think she could have stolen them! I mean, it would be really easy for a dog walker to steal dogs. Nobody would ever suspect her."

Jane rested her chin in her hand and frowned. "I must admit that it *is* a little strange that she only ever seems to have good-looking, pedigree dogs with her."

"And pedigrees are worth more," pointed out Neil as things became even clearer to him. "A dog thief could sell them and make good money."

"But she doesn't *always* walk pedigrees," put in Emily. "Remember she said that the dog she mistook Bagel for wasn't a pedigree?"

"But I wonder if she *did* mistake Bagel for another dog," said Neil, glancing at the glossy black dog stretched out in the center of the living room.

Emily and Jane looked at him, confused.

"I'm beginning to think that she recognized him right away," Neil explained. "And that he recognized her, too. That's probably why he acted up so much when he saw her."

"Just a sec, Neil," said Richard. "I'm not following your argument here."

Neil reminded Richard of what they'd told him about Bagel's bizarre behavior toward Glynnis in Central Park the day before. "When I think about it, it was almost as if he was scared of her. And that could be because she had stolen him from his owner — not because Glynnis had lost him."

"But he was with the taxi driver," said Richard, frowning.

"Yes, but don't you see?" said Neil. "Stan found him *after* Bagel had managed to escape from Glynnis!"

Emily kneeled down next to Bagel and fingered his collar. "If Glynnis *did* steal him, that could explain why he didn't have a name tag," she said. "She would have taken it off so that he couldn't be easily identified."

"I don't know," said Richard, shaking his head. "I think you're reading too much into the situation. After all, what evidence do you have?"

"But do you think it's just a coincidence that

Glynnis said she'd lost a black Lab and Stan found an almost identical one in the same area?" asked Neil.

Richard ran a hand through his hair. "Well, it is a coincidence," he agreed. "But I'm not sure it's enough to prove that she's a thief."

"And she *was* adamant that she didn't know him," Jane reminded Neil and Emily.

"That's because she saw that he recognized us," said Neil. "She had to pretend she'd made a mistake so we wouldn't suspect her of anything."

Jane, deep in thought, looked at Bagel. "A lot of what you say does make sense," she said slowly. "And come to think of it, Glynnis always seems to walk different dogs, whereas I've had the same group ever since I started the job."

"I still think it's far-fetched," said Richard. "A dog thief posing very publicly as a dog walker?" He shook his head. "Sorry, Neil. I think you're wrong this time."

"Look," said Jane, turning to Neil and Emily, "I don't think we can jump to conclusions on the basis of a few coincidences. I've known Glynnis for several months now and, even though she can be unfriendly, she does seem to be doing a good job of walking dogs. Otherwise someone would have caught on to her by now — right?"

Neil shrugged, but before he could reply, the telephone rang. Everyone looked up expectantly, and Neil felt himself become tense. Could this be Bagel's owner responding to the advertisement? Putting aside his suspicions about Glynnis, Neil followed Jane into the hall, where he looked on anxiously as she answered the call.

"Stan!" said Jane. She paused, then said, "No, so far not a single call. But the ad just came out today, and a lot of people haven't seen the paper yet. I'm sure we'll get a response later."

For the rest of the evening, Neil waited anxiously for the call that would claim Bagel. But the only call was from Bob and Carole, seeing how Neil and Emily were doing and letting them know that Jake was fine. Later, lying restlessly in bed, Neil stretched out his hand to pat the Labrador, who was sleeping on the floor between the two beds with Delilah. Bagel had been lost for at least three days now. How could anyone not be missing a terrific dog like him?

CHAPTER SEVEN

Neil held on tightly to Bagel's leash as they threaded their way through the crowds entering the baseball stadium the next evening.

"We don't want you getting lost *again*," he told the Labrador, looping the leash over his hand once more.

Bagel trotted along, completely at ease among the jostling fans. It was almost impossible to believe that this was the same dog that had been so frantic in Central Park the other day.

"We'll go up to the bleachers on that side of the field," said Casey, leading the way. "That's where I normally sit."

"Bleachers?" Emily asked, with a bewildered look on her face.

"Oh — that's baseball terminology. In England, I

think they call it a stand," explained Casey. "I'll have to remember to translate some of the vocab for you two. I guess it could be pretty confusing otherwise."

"Just like cricket can be confusing if you don't know anything about *that* game," said Neil, with a grin.

They found seats halfway up in the bleachers and Neil told Bagel to sit at his feet. The Labrador sat obediently and looked around the stadium with interest, but after a while he became slightly restless. He stood up and leaned over the spectator in front of him, panting heavily next to his head.

"Would you mind controlling your dog, please?" asked the man. "He's drooling on me."

"Sorry," apologized Neil, and he shortened the leash so that Bagel had to sit again.

The buzz of excitement in the stadium grew louder when nine players from one of the teams ran out and stood in a row along one side of the baseball diamond.

"Those are the Mets," said Casey proudly. "They'll field first because they're the home team." She stood up along with everyone else in the bleachers and yelled encouragement to her team. Bagel also leaped to his feet, jerking Neil's arm forcefully, and began to whine and yap. Neil had to hang on to the leash with both hands to restrain the Labrador.

"Sit, Bagel," he shouted firmly. But Bagel ignored him and, straining forward, barked more loudly — right into the ear of the man in front.

The man turned around again and glared at them. Neil mouthed another apology and managed to get the Labrador back under control. Perhaps it hadn't been such a good idea to bring him along after all. All the noise was obviously making him much too excited. Neil began to worry that he'd never be able to keep him quiet throughout the whole game.

The Atlanta Braves then came onto the field, followed by a school choir, which began to sing the American national anthem. Soon everyone in the stadium was singing heartily. Neil hummed along. He wished he knew the words so that he could sing them, too. The singing seemed to have a calming effect on Bagel. He settled down quietly and fixed his eyes on a distant point on the far side of the field.

The moment the singing was over, the Braves returned to their dugout, leaving their first batter on the field. "He's at home plate," Casey explained.

The Mets' pitcher readied himself on the pitcher's mound, then threw the first ball to the batter. The player struck the ball hard, threw down his bat, and made it to first base a split second before an outfielder threw the ball at it. A huge shout broke out from the crowd and Bagel started to squirm and yap again. Neil hung on to the leash grimly, hoping that Bagel wouldn't break free or slip out of his collar.

The Braves scored runs at a steady rate. Eventually, when a batter was called out after missing the ball three times, Casey threw up her arms in delight. "Strike three! Back to the dugout for you!" She beamed as the batter walked off the field and joined the rest of his team on their bench.

Before long, two more of the Braves' batters were out and the teams swapped roles. It was the Mets' turn at bat.

The Braves' pitcher tossed the ball to the first batter, who whacked it so hard that he managed to run all the way around the diamond, past the other three bases and back to home plate.

"Home run!" cheered Casey triumphantly.

Neil and Emily, encouraged by Casey's enthusiasm, rooted energetically for the Mets, too. But the uproar in the stadium made Bagel even more difficult to control. He trembled and bounced with excitement and Neil had to hold on to his collar with both hands to keep him on the ground.

The Mets' score began to mount up. Neil was glad that they were doing well. Perhaps the loss of Joe hadn't dampened the team's spirits after all. It might have made them even more determined to win.

"Oh no!" moaned Casey as a batter swung at a pitch and missed it.

"Strike one!" came a voice over the loudspeaker.

The pitcher threw another ball to the batter, who swung at it but missed again.

"Strike two!" came the amplified voice.

Neil looked at Casey. She had her hand to her mouth and was holding her breath.

The batter swiped wildly at the next pitch. The ball hurtled past him to the catcher and a groan of disappointment came from the Mets' supporters in the crowd.

"Strike three!"

The batter returned despondently to the Mets' dugout on the far side of the field and, from then on, their luck changed for the worse. Within minutes, another batter was walking off the field without scoring a single run.

The next player came out of the Mets' dugout and made his way to home plate. "Let's hope *he* gets to score a few runs," said Casey. "Otherwise we're going to be way behind the Braves."

The batter adjusted his helmet and raised his bat. The pitcher tossed the ball at him and he swung hard, smacking the ball with enormous force. The ball traveled at lightning speed through the air — straight into the glove of an outfielder.

"Darn!" Casey exclaimed in frustration as the player walked off the field. "That's the last thing we needed. The Braves could really pull ahead in the next inning."

The dispirited player had almost made it to the Mets' dugout when Bagel, who had been squirming frantically in Neil's grip, suddenly lurched forward more strongly than before. Neil braced himself and tried to pull him back, but this time the Labrador was too forceful. With a mighty tug he broke away from Neil and, in an instant, he was charging down the bleachers.

"Bagel!" Neil leaped to his feet and scrambled after the Labrador. But by the time he'd made it to the bottom of the steps, Bagel had slipped through the barrier and was galloping straight across the field.

"Someone grab that dog!" shouted a security guard.

Bagel streaked past the umpire and the Braves' fielders, who gaped with astonishment at the frantic dog. One or two players lunged toward him, but the big Labrador neatly sidestepped them and continued to power his way across the field. Howls of laughter came from the stands as the spectators rose to their feet to get a good view of the unexpected change in play.

"This way," shouted Neil to Emily and Casey, who were running behind him. They raced down the side of the field, keeping close to the fence. They couldn't simply go running across the field after Bagel — that was probably against the rules and would really cause a scene. But Neil knew they had to reach the other side as fast as they could before Bagel managed to get into even more trouble. What in the world had gotten into the crazy dog this time?

Bagel had almost reached the far side of the field when a member of the Braves suddenly jumped directly into his path. It was too late for Bagel to duck to one side and the man braced himself, ready to grab the dog. But Bagel was unstoppable. He collided with the player, sending him sprawling to the ground, and, without losing momentum, took off again.

The crowd gasped, but the player rose to his feet, unhurt, and stood with his hands on his hips while he watched the dog bounding away.

Meanwhile, Neil, Emily, and Casey were hurtling around the perimeter of the field. Neil kept his eye firmly on Bagel and willed himself to run faster. "Hurry!" he yelled over his shoulder to Emily and Casey. "We've got to catch him before he disappears into the crowd."

Neil's heart pounded in his chest and his mouth

felt dry. Bagel seemed to be on some kind of urgent mission. What else could explain his weird behavior?

They ducked past vendors, cameramen, and spectators, who had quickly gathered at the fence to get a closer look at the strange goings-on. Then, turning the corner, they ran down the far side of the field, just in time to see Bagel heading straight for the Mets' dugout. Without hesitating, the Labrador leaped into the shelter and disappeared from Neil's view.

"Oh no!" groaned Neil. "Now we're really going to be in trouble." He imagined the dog bowling some of the players over — perhaps even injuring them — then escaping beneath the bleachers, through the gates of the stadium, and out into the busy road beyond.

Out of breath, and with perspiration dripping

from his forehead, Neil approached the dugout almost reluctantly. He was responsible for Bagel and he knew that he would have to take the blame for any damage the dog had caused. But even more upsetting was the thought that Bagel could be lost again — and this time for good.

When they got to the dugout, the sight that met them made Neil blink in astonishment. Instead of the pandemonium he had expected, there were cheers and laughter! And Bagel seemed to be the cause of it.

The Labrador was sitting proudly on the bench, looking as if he didn't have a care in the world. A huge grin stretched across his face, and his thick tail thumped up and down, while the player who had just come off the field hugged him tightly.

"You clever boy," the player was saying. "You found us — and just in time."

Neil recognized the man immediately. In a flash, everything suddenly made sense. The man was Mike Maitland — the player who had appeared on television appealing for his dog. And Bagel was Joe DiMaggio!

"Joe! I should have known." Neil grinned with relief.

"But he *can't* be Joe," argued Emily. "He doesn't have a white star on his chest."

"I bet he does," said Neil. "It's just that we couldn't see it. If we look closely, we'll find it."

"You mean —" began Casey.

"Yep," said Neil. "Someone must have dyed the star to disguise Joe."

The Labrador looked at Neil and barked happily as if agreeing with him, then licked Mike's face vigorously. Neil was thrilled. As Bagel, the dog had been cheerful and friendly, but now, back with his own people, Joe was clearly in his element.

Emily laughed at the sight of the big dog sitting confidently on the bench. "We should have figured it out," she said. "Especially since he was found near Central Park — which is exactly where he got lost in the first place."

"Mmm — we could have saved the team a lot of worry," said Neil.

"Just think — he was right under our noses all along!" Casey laughed.

The players looked at the three of them in surprise. "So you're responsible for Joe's return?" said Mike.

"Well — yes and no," said Neil. "You see, it was really Joe who found *you* in the end —"

"Hey, guys," interrupted a man who, Neil realized, was the team's manager. "It's great to have Joe back, but we can't hold up the game any longer — we're supposed to be on the field right now."

Neil was suddenly aware of loud booing and hissing coming from the crowd. The fans were obviously becoming impatient at the delay.

Grabbing their helmets, the players ran to take their positions on the field. Mike patted the mascot and commanded him to stay, then turned to Neil, Emily, and Casey. "Would you mind staying with him and watching the rest of the game from here?" he asked. "I'd really like to hear the whole story later."

"Would we ever!" Casey beamed as the player ran out to join his teammates.

Neil crouched down in front of Joe and examined the fur on his chest. It didn't take him long to detect a lighter area in the sleek, black coat. He traced the patch with his finger and clearly identified the star shape that was Joe's distinguishing mark.

"Here's the final proof," he said to Casey and Emily, who kneeled down and scrutinized Joe's chest until they, too, could make out the star.

"It's a very good job," said Emily, straightening up. "You have to get really close to see that the fur's been dyed."

The next inning was more successful for the Mets. When it was their turn at bat, they hit the ball so sharply and accurately that runs came quickly. With each run, Joe squirmed with excitement on the bench, and whenever a batter returned to the dugout the mascot would welcome him cheerfully. It wasn't long before the Mets had nearly caught up with their rivals' score.

Casey cuddled Joe. "You *knew* your team needed you," she said. "Just look how they've turned around their game."

At one stage of the game, when Mike returned to the dugout after being up at bat, Neil explained how the Labrador had come to be with them.

"So we have not only you three to thank, but the cab driver, too," said the player. "Do you have his name and number? I'd like to give him a call."

"His name is Stan Schneider," said Neil, and told Mike the name of the cab company.

At the start of the next inning, Joe's owner was about to go out to his field position when a polite cough outside the dugout caught everyone's attention. They turned to see a member of the rival team standing nearby. Joe jumped down from the bench and, with his hackles raised, planted his feet squarely on the ground and glared at the man.

Emily nudged Neil. "Isn't he the one who was on TV the other night?" she whispered.

"Looks like him," agreed Neil.

Casey nodded slowly. "And you know what else?" she said, under her breath. "Look at his number. He's the guy that Joe knocked down when he was running across the field!"

Neil and Emily chuckled quietly. "That's payback for you!" said Emily.

The player took a few steps forward, but a low warning growl from Joe made him stop in his tracks. "OK, Joe, I won't come any closer," he said. "I'll just have my say from here." Joe growled again. "Yes, I know you regard me as the enemy," he said to Joe. Then, addressing the players, he added, "I just want to say, on behalf of my team, that we're thrilled — and relieved — that you have your dog back."

There was an awkward silence for a few seconds until Mike stepped forward and shook hands with his opponent. "No hard feelings," he said, "especially since Joe kind of got back at you by bowling you over in front of all your fans!"

The Braves player laughed. "I guess I deserved that treatment!"

Seeing his owner talking in a relaxed way with his opponent, Joe put down his hackles and trotted forward to sniff at the man's outstretched hand.

"Do you forgive me, boy?" asked the Braves player. Joe's expression softened and the man patted him gently on the head. "I really did try hard to find you when you gave me the slip in the park." Then he glanced over his shoulder. "I'd better be getting back — I'm next at bat."

Joe watched the player running across the field, then he gave a bark, turned, and put out a paw toward Neil.

I think he's giving me a high five, thought Neil with a smile. At the same time, he thought about

how wary the usually friendly dog had been toward Glynnis. That reminded him that they still didn't know for sure who had stolen Joe for the second time and dyed his fur. . . .

A loud cheer from Casey broke into his thoughts. The Braves player struck out. Neil joined her in applauding the Mets and soon he was completely absorbed in the game.

The Mets were now more determined than ever to win, and by the end of the ninth inning the score was tied. Casey chewed her nails in suspense.

"What happens now?" asked Neil. "Do they go into overtime?"

"Yes," Casey nodded.

The extra inning got underway with the Braves batting first. They scored runs quickly and were well ahead again by the time three of their batters were out. Then it was the Mets' turn to bat.

"This is it," said Casey nervously.

The first of the Mets batters took his position at home plate while the rest of the team sat in the dugout, nervously waiting for their turn to bat. Even Joe looked apprehensive. He sat bolt upright, his dark brown eyes fixed firmly on the scene before him.

Slowly, the Mets' score crept up. The players sitting on the bench shouted encouragement to their teammates on the field, but when two batters were called out, one after the other, a gloom began to settle on everyone. The team was still a few runs behind. If another batter struck out, it would all be over and the visiting team would win after all.

The next player at bat was Mike. He got up from the bench and swung his heavy aluminum bat over his shoulder. "I'll do it," he said determinedly. He put his arm across Joe's back. "We'll show them, won't we, boy?" Then he strode across the field to face the pitcher.

Joe jumped off the bench and stood at the edge of the field, watching his owner preparing for the first pitch. The Braves pitcher raised his left leg and was on the point of throwing the ball when Joe let out a loud, urgent bark that echoed around the hushed arena.

Mike let the bat drop. He glanced over at his dog, who was now darting backward and forward behind the line at the edge of the field.

"What's Joe up to now?" asked Neil.

The team manager shrugged. "Who knows? He's never done this during a game before. But we'd better get him to settle down — he's disrupting play again."

"He could be trying to urge Mike on," said Neil, going toward Joe. "Here, boy. That's enough now."

When he heard Neil's voice, Joe immediately sat behind the line, just outside the dugout where his owner could see him. Out on the field, Mike lifted his bat once more. The pitcher threw the ball and, with a powerful swing, Mike whacked it so hard that it soared high into the air and sailed right into the stands.

The crowd rose to their feet and cheered as Mike charged off from home plate and rounded the bases. His home run was a grand slam — because there was a player on every base, it drove in four runs. Casey jumped up and down, clapping her hands in delight. Neil couldn't help laughing at her. This was his first time at a baseball game, but he felt sure that they didn't get more exciting than this.

There was a big celebration in the Mets' dugout. The players hugged Joe ecstatically. "You brought back our luck!" one of the players told the dog, whose face was creased in the biggest doggy grin Neil had ever seen. Joe was lapping up all the attention.

"Yes — nothing like a bit of barking from the sidelines to encourage a guy." Mike laughed. "And if it hadn't been for you three," he said, turning to Neil, Emily, and Casey, "he wouldn't have been here to bring us luck. I'll tell you something else," he added confidently, "we're going to take the Subway Series on Saturday. The Yankees don't stand a chance against us now. Just you wait and see."

"We'll be watching you on TV, holding our breath, so you'd better not let us down!" Casey grinned.

Neil was now sorry there was no chance of getting tickets to the big game.

"We'll do our best not to disappoint you," said the team manager. "Especially since we owe you one for solving the mystery of our missing mascot!"

“But there’s still one part of the mystery that hasn’t been solved,” said Neil.

“What’s that?” asked Mike.

“Joe’s whereabouts from the time he escaped from the Braves to when Stan, the cab driver, found him,” Neil told him.

“We know he was in Central Park the night before Stan rescued him,” said Emily. “The doorman at the Plaza Hotel saw him.”

“OK. But that still leaves a couple of days,” said Neil. He folded his arms and stared into the distance, deep in thought. He had an idea where Joe had been during those two days. But he needed proof. And he was going to have to figure out a way to get it.

"The best part was seeing how happy Joe and his owner were to be together again," said Neil later that evening, when they were back at the Hammonds' house.

They were sitting on the back porch having a late snack before going to bed. Delilah lay quietly by Jane's side, enjoying having her long, sleek coat brushed. When Neil and Emily first came in, the collie had looked around for her Labrador friend. But soon she accepted that he wasn't there anymore and settled back into being a contented single dog.

"So, all's well that ends well," said Richard.

"Um . . . not exactly."

Jane stopped brushing Delilah and looked up. "What do you mean, Neil?"

"We still haven't tracked down Joe's thief," he explained.

Jane and Richard exchanged puzzled looks and Neil quickly added, "The one who must have stolen him from the Braves player in Central Park."

"We don't know that he *was* stolen a second time," said Richard. "And anyway, does it matter anymore? The important thing is that Joe's back."

"Yes, it *does* matter," insisted Neil. "I believe he *was* stolen again, and unless the thief is caught, more pedigree dogs will disappear."

"But how can you be sure Joe wasn't just running loose after he got away from the Braves?" asked Jane.

"Because someone definitely dyed his fur to disguise him," explained Neil.

"Mmm. That's a good point," said Jane. "But if your suspicions *are* correct, where would we even *begin* to look for the thief?"

"In Central Park — where Joe first disappeared," said Neil.

Richard sighed. "Central Park's a very big place, Neil," he said.

"I know. But we do have one lead. And that's Glynnis," said Neil. "I still think she's up to no good."

Richard gave Neil a hard look. "I thought we decided yesterday that you really can't jump to such a conclusion on the basis of very flimsy evidence," he said. "Some ads for a couple of lost dogs that look like the ones Glynnis walks don't prove anything."

"I know," said Neil. "But remember, Joe got very upset when he saw her — and he also got pretty worked up when he saw the man who first stole him. Those are the only people we've ever seen him snarl at. Doesn't *that* make you wonder?" He turned to Jane. "Don't you think it's worth checking up on her?" he pleaded.

"I guess so." Jane sighed, putting down the dog brush. "After all, we *did* see her trying to get hold of him."

"And remember how embarrassed she seemed when she thought he belonged to us," Emily reminded them.

There was a loud rustle in some shrubs at the bottom of the steps. Delilah immediately sat up. She put her head to one side, listening intently for the noise again. When she heard it seconds later, she sped down the steps to investigate.

"Find!" Richard urged her as she started to sniff around in the shrubs.

Neil got up and went to the top of the steps to get a closer look at what Delilah was doing. The collie scratched around in the soil at the base of the shrubs, then flopped to the ground and lay very still, waiting for something to appear in front of her.

Richard returned to the subject of Glynnis. "OK, let's assume that your suspicions are correct. How could you possibly prove that Glynnis stole Joe?"

"We could set her up," said Neil at once. Ever since

he'd discovered that Joe's star had been dyed, he'd been thinking about how to trace the thief.

"Set her up?" Richard frowned.

A sudden sharp yap from Delilah interrupted the conversation. Richard got up and joined her. "What is it, girl?"

Delilah was crouching in her familiar herding position. She stared ahead at something in the center of the lawn. Neil craned his neck, trying to spot what she'd seen. The collie sneaked forward. Neil's eyes became adjusted to the fading light out in the garden and he spotted what Delilah was after — a pair of squirrels scampering around the base of the oak tree.

"Squirrels! She's just doing her job." He laughed quietly.

"You mean, herding the livestock," joked Jane.

Neil watched the black-and-white dog zig-zagging across the yard, her eyes fixed, unblinking, on the squirrels. He'd seen the same strong instinct in Jake. Herding was something a Border collie just couldn't help doing! And it wasn't just sheep that brought out that instinct, either.

Richard went back to his chair. "Luckily, she doesn't stand a chance of getting too close. The squirrels always spot her first." He poured himself a glass of iced tea. "So, exactly how do you intend to set up Glynnis, Neil?"

"We could trick her into trying to steal a dog," said Neil.

"What dog?" asked Jane.

Neil looked across the yard at Delilah, who was now sniffing the tree trunk. The squirrels had made a quick getaway into the safety of the branches above.

"You're not thinking of Delilah?" Jane frowned, following Neil's gaze.

"I am." Neil nodded. "Anyone can see that she's well bred. And she's a very good-looking dog — Glynnis would know that she'd get a lot of money for her. . . . We'd be there to make sure she was safe."

Jane folded her arms. "Well, that goes without saying!"

Neil then outlined his plan to the others. They could take Delilah to Central Park the next day at about the time Jane usually saw Glynnis. As soon as they caught sight of the woman, they'd let Delilah off her leash, then hide and wait to see what Glynnis would do.

"I bet you anything she'll try to get hold of Delilah," finished Neil.

Central Park was alive with activity when they arrived there the next afternoon. Casey had come along, too. She was determined to help trap the woman who had caused her beloved Mets so much anguish.

Jane led them directly to the area of the park where she usually bumped into Glynnis. Neil was on full alert for the first sign of the dog walker. He had to make sure she didn't spot them first. If she did, she'd make no move to snatch the collie.

Delilah walked just ahead of them at the end of her leash. Most of the time, her nose was firmly on the ground, tracking the scent of other dogs that had passed that way earlier.

They passed joggers and cyclists and several other people walking dogs, but there was no sign of Glynnis. Delilah spotted some children playing with a

Frisbee in an open, grassy area, and she started to yap excitedly.

"She'd love to join in," said Jane, holding the leash tightly. "Frisbees are just about her favorite toy."

Delilah's high-pitched bark attracted a lot of attention. "This isn't helping," said Jane. "We wouldn't stand a chance of sneaking up on Glynnis if she showed up now. Let's take that route." She pointed to a path which veered away from where the children were playing.

The path led through clusters of trees and shrubs. Neil hoped that Glynnis would arrive soon — the shrubs would be a perfect place to hide.

His hopes were soon rewarded when they turned a corner and saw Glynnis and two golden cocker spaniels walking briskly along the path about fifty yards ahead of them.

"That's her," hissed Neil, signaling everyone to stop.

"We're going to have to catch up to her without her seeing us," whispered Casey.

At that moment, Delilah began to pull Jane toward a group of squirrels scampering about in a clearing to one side of the path just ahead. Delilah resisted Jane's attempts to pull her back. Her focus was on one thing only. She just *had* to herd those squirrels! Neil couldn't believe their luck. Here was an ideal opportunity for their plan to be put into action.

"Quick!" urged Neil. "Let her go. She might herd them toward Glynnis."

Jane hesitated for a moment. "I hope she'll be all right," she said anxiously.

"She *will* be," said Neil confidently. "I'll make sure of that."

Jane sighed and gave Delilah a quick hug before releasing her. Then the four of them dived for cover behind a group of shrubs.

Just as Neil had expected, the instant the little animals saw the collie coming their way, they scooted off at top speed — in Glynnis's direction. They ran to a small grove of trees and scuttled up the trunks to safety at the very moment Glynnis was walking past. The noise of the squirrels clawing their way up the trunk made her look around, and as she did, she stopped dead in her tracks.

Squinting through the branches and leaves, Neil held his breath. Glynnis had seen Delilah. The striking black-and-white Border collie was crouching at the bottom of a tree, her attention firmly fixed on the squirrels. *An easy target for a dog thief!* Neil thought. From his leafy hiding place, he could even see a sly smile creep across Glynnis's face.

Everything happened very quickly. Glynnis attached the spaniels to a lamppost and looked around furtively, making sure no one was watching. Then she pulled a leash out of her pocket and went straight over to the unsuspecting collie. Delilah, having by now lost interest in the crafty squirrels, became aware of the woman approaching. She stood up and wagged her tail in a friendly greeting.

Jane stifled a gasp. "Careful, Delilah," she whispered.

"It couldn't be easier for her," breathed Emily as Glynnis quickly clipped the leash onto Delilah's collar.

"How *dare* she take advantage of a dog's trust!" Neil muttered angrily.

Glynnis started to pull Delilah along. The collie began to realize that something was wrong, and dug in her heels. She turned around, looking for Jane and the others, and started to whine.

"Move it!" snapped Glynnis. She dragged Delilah toward the spaniels, who looked as miserable and confused as Delilah did.

"I think we've seen enough," said Jane decisively. She burst out from behind the shrubs and sprinted toward Glynnis.

Neil, Emily, and Casey followed hard on Jane's heels.

"Don't you dare take another step with my dog!" shouted Jane.

Glynnis spun around in astonishment. When she saw them all closing in on her, the blood drained from her face. She opened her mouth and tried to speak, but Jane cut her off.

"Don't even bother to deny it. We know exactly what you were up to. You were trying to steal my dog!" She snatched the leash away from Glynnis, and Delilah wriggled with relief around Jane's legs.

"These two dogs are stolen, too, aren't they?" blurted out Neil, pointing to the shivering spaniels.

"I . . . er . . . they're . . ." Glynnis began, but then she just took a deep breath and looked at her feet.

"And they're not the only ones," continued Neil sharply. "You've stolen other dogs so that you could sell them!"

Glynnis raised her head and gave Neil a cold stare. "Who do you think you are, accusing me like that?" she snapped. "What proof do you have?"

Jane stepped forward. "I think the fact that you were trying to steal Delilah would be enough for the police to start an investigation," she said.

"*And* we could find out who the owners of the

spaniels are and speak to them," added Emily, pointing to the name tags on the dogs' collars.

Glynnis sighed. Neil could see that she knew the game was up. "I guess I can't deny taking these dogs," she said in a small voice.

"Or any of the others," insisted Neil.

Glynnis narrowed her eyes at him and said nothing.

Then Neil delivered his next blow. "*And* you stole Joe, the Mets' mascot, didn't you? You even dyed his famous white star to try to disguise him!"

Glynnis swallowed hard. "You can't prove that," she said, her face now red with embarrassment. "What makes you think I did that?"

"Everything adds up," Neil told her. "The dogs were the first ones to give you away."

This surprised Glynnis. "Huh? The *dogs* told you?"

"Well, they all acted so crazy around you — especially Joe!" Neil declared. "He was never like that with any other people — even strangers — so I knew you must have done something to make him like that."

"We could see that he recognized you," explained Emily. "So when you said you'd made a mistake and he wasn't yours, we got suspicious."

"And when we realized that Bagel was Joe, and that someone had stolen him from the Braves player, we figured it must have been you," Neil went on. "You disguised him by dyeing his fur, but Joe got away from you, and when you saw him again you tried to grab him."

Glynnis glared at him icily.

"Luckily for Joe, we saw it all," said Jane.

"I didn't steal him from the Braves," protested Glynnis. "I . . . er . . . I . . ." she began, then added quickly, "I heard about him on the news and was only trying to get a hold of him to take him back to the Mets and claim the reward."

Jane shook her head. "Sorry, Glynnis, but we don't believe you. You're forgetting that Joe already knew you."

"Nobody else knows that," retorted Glynnis.

Jane gave a little smile. "I'm sure that with all the evidence we have already, our story is more likely to be believed than yours."

Glynnis shook her head. "I guess I should have known I'd never get away with stealing such a famous dog," she said.

"Or *any* dogs, for that matter," Jane reproached her. "Have you, for one minute, thought about how much heartache you've caused?"

Glynnis shuffled her feet and mumbled, "It just seemed like a good way to make money."

A wave of anger passed through Neil. To think that she cared so little for the dogs! But at least she'd been found out. That would put an end to her cruel ways.

As if she'd read his thoughts, Glynnis gave him another cold stare. "Too bad you know so much about dogs," she grumbled. "Otherwise, I might have gotten away with it."

Jane took her cell phone out of her bag. "Well, now that you've confessed to us," she said, dialing a number, "you can repeat your story to the police."

Glynnis looked thoroughly defeated. She sat on the bench and stared at the ground in humiliation. Neil felt a moment's pity for her, but quickly brushed it aside. Now that Glynnis had been found out, dogs would be a lot safer in Central Park.

The next morning they were all getting ready for a trip to a beach on Long Island when the phone started to ring.

"I'll get it," called Neil, who was on his way upstairs to get his swim trunks.

A few minutes later he joined the others, grinning mysteriously.

"What's up, Neil?" asked Jane putting some cans of soda into a cooler. "You look like you're up to something."

"You won't believe this," he said.

They all looked at him in anticipation.

"We're going to the game tonight!"

"*The* game? You don't mean the Subway Series final?" Richard asked in disbelief.

"Yes." Neil nodded. "The very same one."

"But that's not possible," said Jane. "Every seat was booked months ago."

Neil smiled. "Well, there's still room for us. *And* — wait till you hear this. . . ." he said, pausing so that the suspense could mount up. "We're going to be the guests of honor!"

"Guests of honor?" Jane echoed.

Neil told them about the telephone conversation he'd just had with the manager of the Mets. The team wanted to thank everyone for taking care of Joe, so they were inviting them all, including Casey, to the game. "He's even sending a car to pick us up!"

"That's amazing!" Emily exclaimed. "I'll run next door to tell Casey."

Jane and Richard were amazed by the news, too. "Wait until my colleagues hear about this," Richard grinned. "They'll be green with envy."

"Just shows what can happen if you're nice to a dog," said Jane. "But I wonder where they'll find seats for us?"

"They'll squeeze us in somewhere — even if it's in their dugout!" Richard laughed. He looked at the clock on the wall. "Come on, guys. We'd better get a move on if we want to get back from the beach in time."

"Our car's here," called Neil when he heard honking in the street outside the house later that day. He opened the front door and saw a brand-new yellow taxi parked at the bottom of the driveway.

"I didn't think they'd send a cab," said Emily.

"Probably the easiest thing to do," said Richard, locking the door once they were all outside.

"Could be a tight fit — all five of us in one cab," said Casey, joining them. "I hope the driver won't mind."

With that, the driver poked his head out of the window. "Where to?" he asked.

Neil's jaw dropped. "Stan!" he exclaimed. "What are you doing here?"

"Picking you up for the big game." Stan grinned.

"But how did you know?" asked Jane.

"The Mets asked me — they've invited me, too!" Stan got out of the taxi and opened the back door. "Four in the back, and you, Neil, can join me up front." He winked. "Plenty of room there now."

Neil smiled at Stan's indirect reference to Joe. "I didn't think you'd be back on the road so soon after the crash," he said.

Stan patted the side of the cab. "Brand-new cab," he said. "Courtesy of my boss."

"You mean he wasn't mad about the accident?" Emily asked.

"He was until he learned that the dog in question was the team's missing mascot," said Stan. "Now he treats me like a hero!"

They all piled into the cab and before long they arrived at Shea Stadium.

"This way," said an official, ushering the little group through the surging crowds. He led them up some stairs and through a door.

"Wow," gasped Neil at the sight that met them. "I feel like a VIP!"

The door opened onto a balcony which provided a bird's-eye view of the entire stadium. There were six reserved chairs on the balcony and on each one was an official Mets baseball cap signed by all the team members. The autographs even included Joe's paw print. Neil was delighted. There couldn't be a better souvenir of his trip to New York.

Loud, stirring organ music heralded the arrival of the two teams on the field. The crowd went wild as the Yankees ran out.

Then came the Mets — headed by a very proud Joe. A thundering cheer broke out as soon as the spectators caught sight of the famous dog. Neil could see how much the Labrador loved all the excitement and attention. He strutted along confidently, looking every inch a champion. "Isn't he just great?" Neil grinned.

Live pictures of Joe flashed across a giant TV screen as he paraded before the many thousands of people. Then, at Mike's command, he sat down below the balcony where Neil and the others were sitting. The player looked up at them and waved. Then, over the loudspeaker, a voice said, "We welcome back a real celebrity — the Mets' famous mascot — Joe!"

When he heard his name, the Labrador stood up and barked at the crowd.

"It looks like he's saying he's glad to be back," said Emily.

"Or that his team will win today," Casey said with a grin.

The Mets then took their positions on the field and their manager quickly led Joe off to the dugout.

"Play ball!" shouted the umpire, and a batter from the Yankees went to stand at home plate, waiting for the first pitch to be thrown to him.

The game was close right from the start and with each ball struck, the atmosphere in the enormous stadium became more electric. Soon Neil was almost hoarse from cheering on the Mets.

At the end of the seventh inning, there was a pause in play.

"Halftime?" Neil asked Casey.

“Not exactly,” she said. “There’s no real break in play — just a pause now when we all get to sing ‘Take Me Out to the Ball Game.’ It’s fun, you’ll see.”

Behind them, they heard the door opening. They turned to see Mike stepping onto the balcony. With him was Joe, who let out a delighted yelp the minute he recognized everyone. He ran up and down in front of the seats, greeting his friends joyfully. When he got to Neil, he jumped up and, with his front paws on Neil’s lap, gave him his trademark welcome of a big wet lick across the face.

Neil laughed and put his arms around the dog’s

neck. "You looked fantastic on the field, boy. Your team must be really proud of you."

"You're not kidding!" Mike chuckled. "There's no better mascot in the game."

An announcement came over the loudspeaker. "I think you guys should listen to this," said Mike, with a smile.

"I'd like to introduce you to some special guests we have today," said the announcer. "Will you all please give a big New York City welcome to Joe's rescuers?"

A bright spotlight fell on the balcony. There was a sudden hush around the huge stadium.

Neil and the others looked at each other in amazement. "I wasn't expecting this!" he said, his eyes wide with surprise.

"Please wave to the crowd," Mike urged them.

"This is a bit embarrassing," protested Jane, waving shyly to the spectators.

The crowd responded with loud applause. Then the announcer explained that the reward for the safe return of Joe would be handed out. With that, the Braves player who had originally taken Joe came up to the balcony and gave Neil and Stan an envelope each.

Neil gasped when he opened the envelope and saw the amount printed on the check. "We can't take all this money," he said. "After all, Joe was no trouble and we didn't really find him — he found us."

"Except after the accident, when he ran off into

Central Park," Emily reminded her brother with a chuckle.

Stan was stunned, too. "Neil's right. We can't take the money. But I know what we *can* do with it."

"You're going to say we should give it to a charity, aren't you?" Neil said to Stan.

"Right on!" said the driver. "And I wonder if you're thinking of the same charity I am?"

"It's got to be the animal shelter where you nearly took Joe," Neil said, smiling.

"We make a great team!" Stan laughed. "We should go into business together!"

Loud organ music filled the stadium again. It was the cue the spectators had been waiting for. Within seconds, tens of thousands of voices joined together to sing "Take Me Out to the Ball Game." Neil listened in awe as the voices surged in unison. It was an experience he knew he'd remember for a very long time.

As soon as the singing ended, Joe's owner put on his cap. "Got to go," he said. "Will you keep Joe with you?"

"You bet!" exclaimed Neil.

The rest of the game was very tense. The teams were so evenly matched that Neil began to think it would be impossible for one of them to win. As in the exhibition game a few days earlier, the game had to run into extra innings. The Mets were the last to bat and the scores were so close that the game could go either way.

"He's got to hit a home run," said Richard as a batter came out.

The batter approached the plate and raised his bat. A deep silence descended on the stadium. Neil bit his lip. This could be the pitch to end it all.

The throw was fast and direct. The batter swung hard at the ball. A loud crack echoed around the stadium and a huge cheer erupted as the ball sailed high into the air and landed up in the balcony — right at Joe's feet!

"Grand slam!" screamed Casey in delight as the batter and the runners on the other bases charged home. "Four runs. We win! The Mets win the Subway Series!"

Neil agreed. "They're the best at baseball, all right." He put his arm around Joe, who was standing up on his hind legs with his front feet on the railing. "And as for you, Joe, you're the best baseball mascot — you're top dog!"